# CHEE-KEE
## A Panda in Bearland

Sujean Rim

LITTLE, BROWN AND COMPANY
NEW YORK  BOSTON

Bearland is a great country that lies across a vast ocean.

The citizens of Bearland are special bears indeed.

Bearland's families and friends work as hard as they play.

Bearland is welcome to all.

"Wow. What did you say?" asked a great brown bear.

"Oh, that is how we say 'peace and happiness,'" explained the new visitor. "I am Mr. Loo. This is Mrs. Loo, and our son, Chee-Kee Loo. We traveled across the ocean from the Island of Coney to live in this great land of yours."

meet you, LOO family."

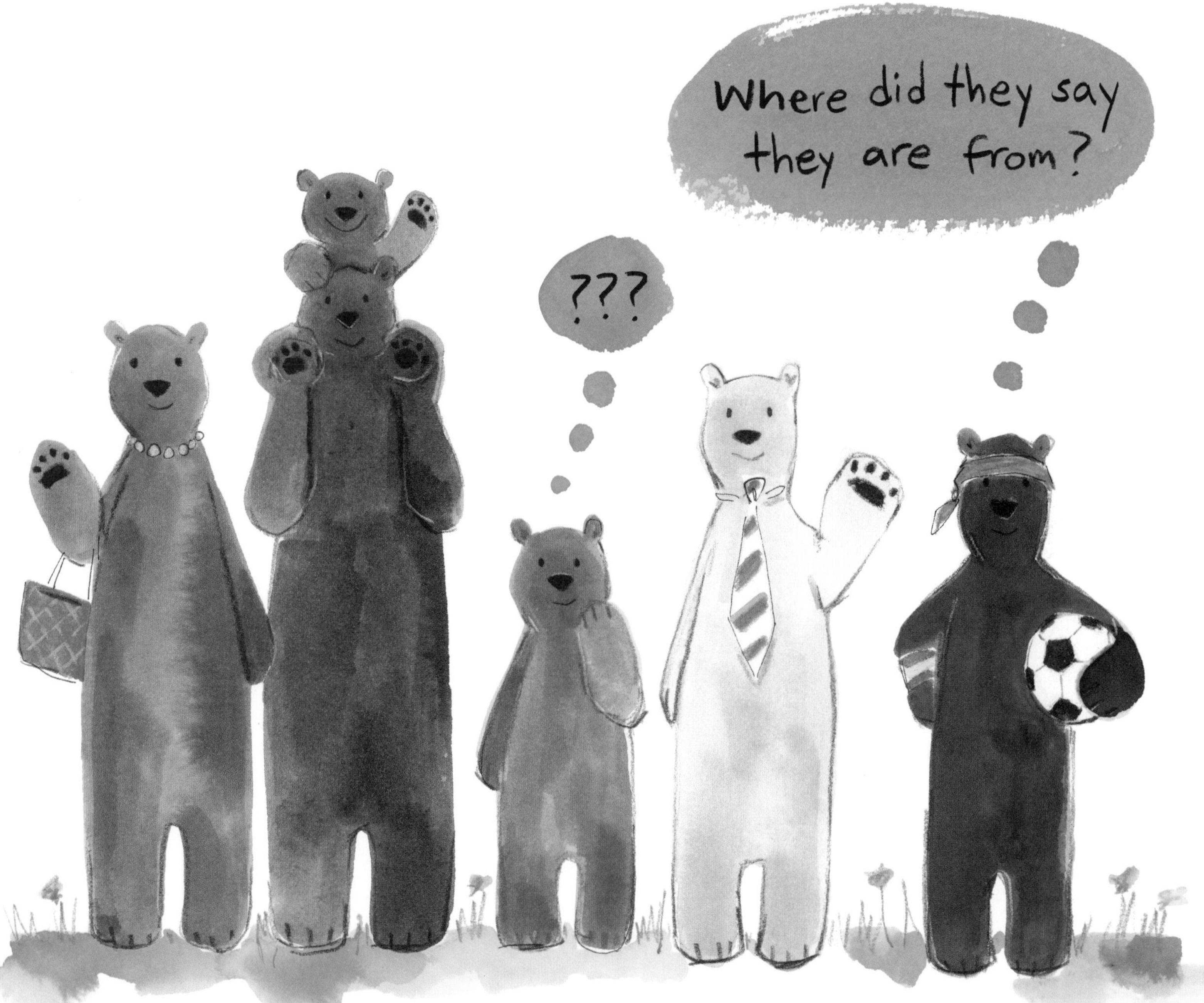

Even though Bearland was very different and they would miss the Island of Coney, Mr. and Mrs. Loo felt so fortunate to be able to come and make a new home in Bearland.

But Chee-Kee felt like he might never feel at home.

He wanted to be just
like everyone else.

But he couldn't help noticing
that he was just so...
different.

When a little bear cub pointed and cried,

"You look funny!"

Mrs. Loo said, "Oh, thank you. You look funny,
too! How lovely."

The Loo family continued on their way.

Chee-Kee thought he would be more comfortable if he wasn't noticeable.

But it seemed that trying to be less noticeable was impossible.

So Chee-Kee went to his favorite spot...alone.

As he watched a big soccer game being played nearby,
he felt even more alone.

And then...

OH NO!

Chee-Kee got to work.

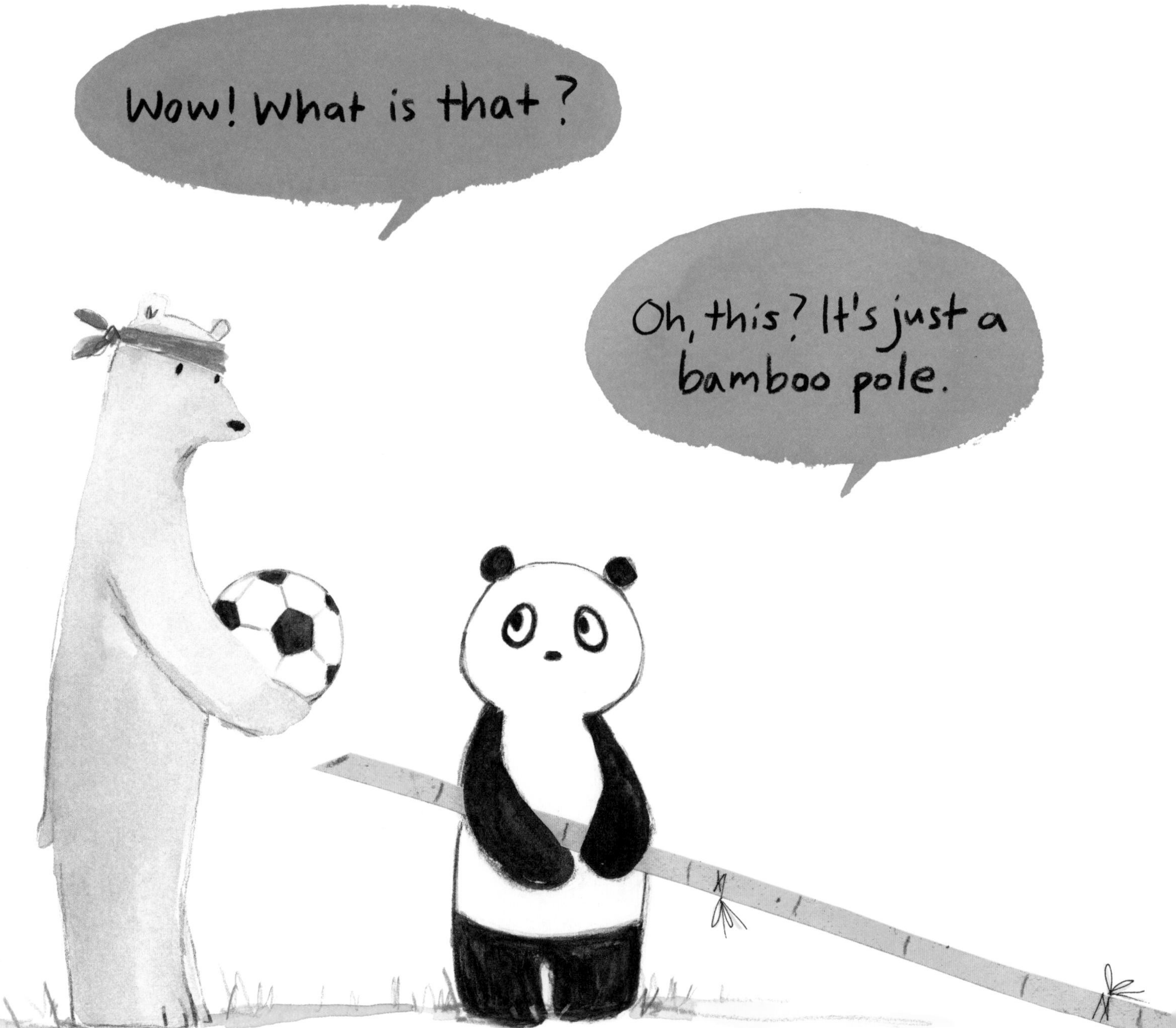
Wow! What is that?
Oh, this? It's just a bamboo pole.

Bearland is a great country with very special bears indeed.

# Author's Note

When I was little, I didn't like being asked "What are you?" and "Where are you from?" because it made me feel like I didn't really belong. I would answer, "I'm from here. I'm an American born in Brooklyn."

I just wanted to fit in.

But when I began to think about my parents immigrating to the United States, I realized how easy I had it.

My mom and dad were born and raised in South Korea, and like so many others, they believed in the American dream. They loved what this country stood for and had faith that coming to America would make their lives better, and make their children's futures brighter.

My dad was in the 1960 and 1964 Olympics; he was a discus and hammer thrower, and he was pretty good. So when he was among a group of international athletes invited to participate in a US-sponsored athletic program, he jumped at the opportunity. And in 1967, my parents packed up their lives, took about five different connecting flights, and moved to the United States of America.

Life was an adjustment, to say the least.

They moved around a bit for various job opportunities, and without another Korean soul in sight, they had a lot to learn on their own. My parents not only looked different and hardly spoke English, but they came with an entirely different set of traditions.

"What are you?" and "Where do you come from?" were accompanied with "Can't you speak English?" and "Don't you know how to do this?" They endured lots of stares and even some spying by curious neighbors. As you can imagine, it wasn't always comfortable. But no matter how lost they felt and how confusing it was just to go grocery shopping (where was the kimchi aisle?), my mom and dad hung in there.

Sure, there were some hard times and tears of frustration, but they made a home for themselves, and they did it by being true to who they are. I am so proud of them.